# *If I Only Knew Then, What I Know Now*

# If I Only Knew Then, What I Know Now

By

*Lois Dais-Kelley*

Publishing Consultant:

Deborah M. Smart
dmsmart@gladstonepublishing.com
http://www.gladstonepublishing.com

Mentioned in the story is **Avon** ®  A perfume
company for women - http://www.avon.com

Publication Date: March 2012

Made in United States

ISBN-13: 978-1-928681-26-7
ISBN-10: 1-928681-26-3

# *Dedication*

I dedicate this book to the life, love and legacy of my parents:

> The Late Mr. and Mrs. Hampton A. Dais

And In Memory of:

> Mr. Oscar Deas (Uncle George)

> Mr. John Dais (Cousin Punch)

Most of all to my home base church family:

> The Greater Bethel Church of Christ

> (Under the leadership of the Late Bishop Herbert Frazier)

# Introduction

The story you are about to read came about due to one word, Obedience. For this story came to me as I was being driven back to New Jersey after being absolutely mesmerized by the gospel play "Woman Though Art Loose" at the Apollo Theater written by Bishop T.D. Jakes.

I found myself being engulfed with words. So I just started writing inside my Bible, on tissue and on any piece of paper I could find. And I continued to expand on this story of words until I reached my home. For this is where the real work with these words truly excelled at an even a greater pace.

Today knowing that I have seen this project through its birthing process is only due once again to my obedience.

I am so very grateful to the Father for allowing me to be a vessel used by Him. So today if you have a desire, a vision, or a dream concerning a story I challenge you to let go and let God.

Be Obedient. And just write.


*Lois Dais Kelley*

# Acknowledgments

First and foremost I give honor to my Lord and Saviour for allowing me to have a career that is truly gratifying and to allow the passion of making a difference in the lives of both my clients, co-workers and parishioners alike. I consider it a blessing to be able to mentor, minister and to be a motivational speaker on a daily basis.

There are so many people to thank but I personally need to thank Patricia Frierson who compelled me to stop sitting on this story and do something with it. I took your advice Pat...thanks for the push! To Wanda Gray who took me to the first book signing of Shontel Thomas (author of "Believe Again!"). Who then in turn introduced me to my publishing consultant, Deborah Smart, whose trust in me was overwhelming from our first conversation, and she continues to be the best business partner, mentor and friend any writer should want in their corner.

To my director Henry Kowal and all my co-workers of Harbor House – thank you for believing in me – it truly means so much to know of your undying faith.

To my friends Eva Byrd, Marguerite Hinton-Taylor, Ruby Johnson and Ann Smalls-thank you for keeping the laughter of all our memories alive and well. Lord knows we've had many to give account for.

Special thanks to my many family members who encouraged me thru this process- Prissana Drakeford (attorney), Dr. Jeanette Deas, Alberta Deas, Katherine McPherson, and John Drakeford.

To my mentor with appreciation, Reverend Connie Coleman.

To the following organizations:

- Passaic County African American Women
- 100 Plus Delta Sigma Theta
- and the NAACP.

A warm shout out and loads of thanks to my photographer Ahleir of Jah's Photo Creations for a job well done.

Last, but not least, my wonderful daughters Verna Kelley and Michelle Dais-Harvey. I thank God for you every day being blessed to be your mother is the single most wonderful thing that ever happened to me. And to my grandchildren Markeith, Doinnell, and Nakuwa you are the song that my heart beats to each and every day.

# *If Only...*

# Introduction

Octavia finds her grandmother in her bedroom sitting in her favorite rocking chair by the window. "Grandma, I'm here to help you pack. What are you doing?"

The elderly lady looks up from the photo album she's been looking through and smiles, "Child, these are all my memories. I'm just revisiting them today."

Octavia smiles and teases, "Memories, Grandma your memories sure do make you look happy."

Her grandmother smiles and shakes her head. "Well, that's because it's all I have of my mother, my sister Matty, and my best friend Asia and her twin sister, Africa."

"Is it true that Aunt Matty and your friends all use to sing together?" She asked sitting on the bed beside her grandmother.

"Sing? Child, we did more than sing child we sang and what more we sang all over and travelled, and made a few demos as well," Grandmother laughed; her eyes just shining with memories.

Touching her album photo, she shook her head and whispered, "They're all dead now."

Octavia felt her grandmother's sorrow and wanted to erase it. "Please tell me about Grandma Auddie, Aunt Matty and your friends, the twins."

"Well, it all started a long, long time ago. We sang in our church choir and we were good! But I'll start with Grandma Auddie; you have to understand her story before hearing about us girls."

# Part I
# Miss Australia Williams

# Chapter One

On a cold wintry evening in Charlotte, North Carolina, nurse Audrey Singleton was carrying a couple's bundle of joy to meet them for the very first time, since the mom's very difficult labor ended with a caesarian operation. As the hospital room door opened, Hank and Claudia Williams' eyes filled with tears at the meeting of their first child, a baby girl.

Nurse Audrey assisted Claudia in shaping her arms to receive her baby as Hank looked on with anticipation of his turn to hold his daughter for the first time. Nurse Audrey smiled and gave support to this couple when Hank asked, "Nurse, your accent is it from the country known as the 'Land Down Under'?"

"Yes," Audrey responded. "I'm from Australia."

"Babe, remember our very first date at the County Fair when I won a Koala Bear for you? And how I always said that's one place I'd like to travel to one day?"

"Sure, I remember," Claudia smiled remembering as she responded.

"Well, what about naming the baby Australia? Auddie for short."

"Our folks will think we've lost our minds Hank, but you know what? I like it. Hmm…Australia Lynette Williams. I like it very much Hank."

Australia was given the world and her parents doted on her effortlessly. But when Auddie was five her parents went out to a New Year's Eve party held by the Rotary Club of Charlotte, and upon leaving they were hit by a drunk driver, and as a result both Hank and Claudia died.

Claudia had a little saying in which she would say to Auddie every time she left for work, or when dropping Auddie off to school; "I love you today and when we're apart, I will love you until we meet together again...Always and Forever."

But for now there was no coming back from *always and forever* and Auddie was placed in her Grandma William's custody and among uncles who would sneak into her room at night. As they would have their way with her, and as this precious child prayed for her parents to take her out of this place for now, it seemed always and forever was taking much too long.

Grandma Williams sensed a change with Auddie as did her teachers. Auddie became so clingy to her grandmother that she even began sleeping with her; for she was too afraid of sleeping in her room by herself and too afraid of saying why.

It was after her grandmother tucked Auddie into her bed one Saturday night, that she noticed her two sons sneaking into Auddie's room. Grabbing her gun, she gave everyone three minutes to get out of her home or find themselves full of bullets, and even if she missed once...somebody was bound to get hit as she yelled, "Now who feels lucky enough to play with me?"

As she aimed her gun to fire, the young men gathered some things and ran as fast as they could in fear of losing their own lives. Grandma Williams stood firm with gun in hand as she watched the young men she raised as her sons run and stumble over each other until they were out of sight.

As Grandma Williams made her way upstairs, Auddie laid in her grandmother's bed still asleep. Grandma kissed her forehead and quietly said, "No one will ever hurt you again as long as I have breath in my body. Please believe me! "And she meant every word.

# Chapter Two

Auddie became the President of the Young People's Summer Seminars, and the Pastor Rev. Kendrick Nelson, Sr. also made her Director of the Youth choir, and The Young People's Meetings; and everyone loved Auddie. The Pastor's son Kenny was also smitten with her charm, her humor and the way she loved the Lord. He was always with her supporting all her efforts as well. They were an item both in and out of school, at church events and; they even occasionally had dinners at each other's homes.

Auddie, being the cheerleader, was always there to support her friend Kenny whether it was at the basketball meets or the football games. But it was at the Youth Championship Bowling League that Kenny asked Auddie to the Prom, and along with that to be his girlfriend.

Finally with only a few days away from the Prom, the shopping was done. All the shopping for gowns and matching the right accessories; all the purchases of hair books to find just the right look; she needed to be at her best with Kenny as her escort. And all of this was worth it because Auddie and Kenny were the talk of the town. Everyone was planning to be near, just to see this young couple off for their first official date to the prom.

It was no surprise that Auddie and Kenny were selected as King and Queen that night, but it was after the prom that Kenny asked the limo driver to drive to the Palace Hotel. And it was that night that Auddie gave her virginity to the young man who made her feel loved all night long and she never wanted the night to end.

With the prom over, Auddie and Kenny watched the mail everyday with the anticipation of being excited for the one college each had dreamt of for such a long time. Even so, although they both had a "favorite" they promised not to reveal it until they received just the right one they were looking for.

"Okay, who did you hear from today Kenny?" Auddie asked.

"New York and Columbia. How about you?" Kenny asked.

"Well, I heard from Dartmouth and Temple," she responded.

"Any of them your favorite choice?" he asked.

"No," Auddie responded holding the phone a little tighter.

Kenny sensed her disappointment, but continued to say trying to reassure her, "But there's still tomorrow."

"You've got that right," she said smiling. "Don't worry tomorrow they'll come

14

and we'll both be celebrating. Gotta go, Grandma's calling. Good night Kenny, love ya!"

"Love you back," Kenny said before hanging up.

Auddie hadn't been feeling well but pushed her way to attend the Youth Bowling League anyway. For she needed to show Kenny her letter of acceptance from the college she'd been waiting to hear from for so long. And, he said he needed to share some news as well. Their team lost as Auddie felt she must be coming down with the flu and that was the reason she wasn't bowling at her best.

When everything was over, Auddie and Kenny went to the Hot Grill for a bite to eat and while waiting for their food each pulled out their acceptance letters and handed them to the other. At the completion of reading each other's letter Auddie started screaming for Auddie was accepted to Spelman, and Kenny was accepted to Morehouse.

With graduation over, everyone was working their full time jobs at the mall in preparation for their college life in the fall. However, Auddie's stomach flu continued to the point she was either late or absent at her position at Lily's Boutique. Grandma Williams met her one Wednesday evening and took her to Dr. Gray, the family physician for years, only to find Auddie was seven weeks pregnant.

Auddie was crying until her grandmother pressed the bell for the bus driver to let them off at the next stop. Auddie said, "Grandma, we're getting off too soon. This isn't our stop."

"Oh yes it is. We're going to the Pastor's house," her grandmother answered.

"No, Grandma, please don't do it this way," Auddie pleaded grabbing onto her grandmother's arm.

"Baby, there is no other way to do it, but face the music here and now," Grandmother Williams took Auddie's hand in hers and continued walking.

When Jenny answered the door, the housekeeper to the Nelson family, she brought them to the Pastor's living room to wait for him; as he was on a very important conference call in his study.

As the Pastor ended his call he pressed the intercom and called for Jenny; which could be heard throughout the eight bedroom mansion. Jenny, a native of Trinidad made her way to the study at which she informed him, Sister Williams and her granddaughter were waiting to see him.

"Come in Sister Williams. How are you and Auddie? We're all so proud of your accomplishments. Auddie, Kenny told us that Spelman has selected you...such good news. And you'll be just a short distance from my Kenny who's attending Morehouse this fall...you know."

"Well Pastor, that's why we're here because we just left the doctor's office," Grandma Williams said.

"Good...good," said the Pastor getting those medical papers back in a timely fashion good for you. Kenny's mom is taking care of that. I believe he's seeing Dr. Short later this week as well."

"No, Pastor. I'm here, no we're here because Auddie is pregnant by your son."

"Now, you just wait one moment here. Let's get one thing straight Sister Williams. I've had 'the talk' with my son and the importance to wrap it up," said the Pastor.

"Well apparently while you were so busy talking, he wasn't listening and the results are he fertilized my granddaughter."

"I've told him before if he lies down with dogs he'll get up with fleas maybe you should've been doing that talk with Auddie. Let me put this in perspective better for you Sista--if you feel my son is responsible for your granddaughter's pregnancy she will not be allowed to do anything at my church *ever!*"

"Wait a minute Pastor, you can't just put her out after all she's done."

"Listen Williams," Pastor Kendrick straightened his back and pointed his finger at Mrs. Williams' face. "Let me help you understand this better. So let me be very clear about this one more time. Take your whorish granddaughter and her lies and get out of my house."

He went on to say, as he stood to usher them out of this office, "Whether it be ten days or ten years from now, she will never be welcome into my church...no matter what!"

Grandma Williams reminded him how much they both had come to love that church in all their years serving the Lord there. Rev. Nelson stood his ground and said, "Well, you can go with her too."

As Grandma Williams stood, she grabbed Auddie and headed for the door, but before she left, she turned and said, "I thought I was worshipping in the House of the Lord. I thought forgiveness was what we practiced here."

"Well you thought wrong. Especially when it affects my family! Now for the last and final time... Get out!"

# Chapter Three

Auddie became quite depressed from the outcome between Pastor Nelson and her grandmother and found herself comfortable in the confines of her room where her pillow held the tears she shed, as it also shielded her from the harsh words that the Pastor said about her and her grandmother.

As the fall weather entered with leaves turning colors before falling, Auddie found herself more alone and depressed than anyone would know, and her only friend and companion was her beloved grandmother. Before her friends left for college, Denise to Mercer County for Mortuary; Sandra to UCLA for acting; Grace to St. John's for Journalism; Clara to South Carolina University for Computer Science; and Millie to Jacksonville State University for Pre-Med, they gave her a baby shower. But, the guilt and shame Auddie was undergoing was so terrifying that she could not face her friends and would not come out of her room.

Now with all of her friends off to their perspective colleges, Auddie felt more abandoned than ever. Having all her efforts to reach Kenny blocked as his cell number was changed, as well as the house phone which now blocked any incoming calls from her as well. So Auddie had no choice but to try to reach out to him once he arrived at Morehouse. "Truly he couldn't be as cold and heartless as his dad," she thought.

She finally found a number to one of the lobby's to the men's dorm and called. The person who answered looked through several forms to connect Auddie to just the right dorm; however, when he returned to the phone and informed Auddie of his findings....it was not what she expected. "Hello, Miss...we have no such name listed in any of our dorms or apartments."

"But, he must be there. He's on a scholarship there. Please look again sir! His name is Kendrick Nelson Jr.," a frantic Auddie responded.

"Wait a minute, are you talking about the minister's son?"

"Yes, that's him," Auddie responded.

"Well Miss, he won't be attending here this year his father had him transferred to NYU," the kind voice relayed.

"Oh no!" screamed Auddie. "That just can't be!"

"I'm afraid so young lady. Sorry I have another call. Good-bye," he said and hung up.

Auddie held the phone which seemed like hours, reliving every word that was spoken. So the loneliness of depression continued to grow, and it continued to worsen on a daily basis.

# Chapter Four

Lisa Nanette Williams was born to an overly stressed and a very much depressed Auddie. She held onto her baby for much of that day after her birth as she wondered, "How am I going to make it now?"

But there was always Grandma Williams, who would remind her to "Stop doubting yourself because God will make a way somehow you just have to trust and believe. Oh yes! Oh yes, He will!"

When Stella Week stopped by to check on Auddie after she came home from the hospital, she said, "Girl give me a comb. Let me try to make a peace treaty with this hair of yours. Why it looks like you're in a war zone!"

"I feel like I'm in a war zone Stel," Auddie said as she broke into tears.

"Okay, we'll have none of that today lady," the most stylish hairdresser in town would say. "Sure, you're hurt, feeling like your heart is beating so fast it scares you, but ladybug, listen to Stella now. In spite of how you may be hurting, you must never let them see you sweat. So dry your eyes girly we have work to do, bottles to make, diapers to purchase, diapers to change and a bassinet to put together. But first let Stel do her best magic trick on your head. Why girl it looks like crows fighting."

"I thought you said it was a war zone?" Auddie tried to laugh sitting back and giving into Stella's gentle touch.

"Your hair lady is all of the above now sit back and hand over that comb!"

After all the work was done, and just before Stella left, she opened her Gucci purse and handed Auddie a bottle of Seagrams.

"Here take a sip of this it will help ease some of your pain, I promise."

Auddie took a sip. "Yeah, I think it will," She thought to herself before taking a second and then a third sip. "I think it will."

As days turned into weeks and the weeks into months, little Lisa was truly growing very nicely, and Grandma Williams was doing her best to work as a domestic a few days a week, as well as, doing laundry for families on the weekends to make ends meet. Auddie was working as a cashier in one of the largest supermarket chains in Charlotte, and with the Christmas holidays approaching she was working more hours to make sure baby Lisa had everything a baby could want.

Yet, one cold wintry evening, Stella drove Auddie and the baby to the mall to finish up some of their last minute shopping when they walked into Mrs. Nelson, who hugged Auddie and kissing the baby said, "She's just beautiful Auddie." Hugging her again she said, "I'll always be near." She pressed something into Auddie's hand. When Auddie looked into her hand, three crisp one-hundred dollar bills were there along with Kenny's phone number.

Pacing in her room after feeding and bathing the baby was all she could do while holding on to the small piece of floral stationary that Mrs. Nelson gave to her. Finally she picked up the phone, pressed it to her heart before placing it to her ear and then started dialing. As her mind repeated statements from..."Why Kenny – Why are you ignoring me?" to "What the hell do you think you're doing? You're a father for goodness sake." And just as she had just the right words to say...Kenny answered the phone.

"Hello Ken here," there was a pause, "Hello, Ken here, speak!"

"Hello Kenny...it's me Auddie."

"Auddie...Listen it's not what you think none of this should have gone down like this. It was all my dad's idea. I can just imagine what you must think of me," said Kenny not knowing what to really say.

"No Kenny, you really don't know or you would've contacted us by now," explained Auddie.

"It's my Dad. I'm sorry. But I do want to see our baby...can I?" He asked.

"Sure," Auddie responded.

"I'll be home for the holidays for about a month, and I promise to tell you everything, if you give me a chance," Kenny responded.

# Chapter Five

Stella as putting the finishing touch on Grandma Williams' hair so she could get to the church on time and find a decent seat for the Christmas Eve Services at her new church; while Auddie was putting baby Lisa to sleep after giving her a nice warm bottle, and giving her a bath and putting on clean pajamas.

"Girl, you out did yourself this time Ms. Stella. I look good tonight you truly know how to work that comb young lady," an excited Grandma Williams said.

Stella responded with a laugh, "Now you know that's right, Ms. Williams."

"Okay I'll see you ladies later. Look after my baby Auddie."

"Of course, Grandma."

"Okay girly out with this hot news you've got me over here for," Stella inquired.

"Kenny's coming over here tonight."

"Kenny? Are you kidding?"

"No Stella, he's home for the holidays and he's coming over in a few to see me and the baby so tighten me up," Auddie responded.

"Okay, anything for you, but please be careful Auddie, 'cause to me he's as shady as his father," Stella warned.

No Stel he's not and after tonight we'll both be okay.  You just watch and see," Auddie assured her.

"Can a tiger change his stripes? No! So be careful. That's all I'm saying," was Stella's last words on the subject.

Auddie continued to look for just the right outfit with Stella's help and later made

sure the house and even the dinner she prepared was in good taste when Kenny arrived.

The phone rang and Auddie was hop-
ing it was Kenny, but it was Grandma
Williams telling Auddie that three persons
would be baptized, and after they cleaned
up around the church her new pastor and
his wife, Reverend Benjamin Hopewell and
Mrs. Hopewell, were taking all the mothers
of the church out to eat, and that she would
be late coming home.

"Oh don't worry Granny, we'll be just
fine. Enjoy yourself," as they ended their
call, the phone rang again. Granny must've
forgotten to tell me something else, Auddie
thought. But when she answered the phone
it was Kenny and he was already outside
parking.

When the doorbell finally rang
Auddie counted to ten before answering,

and there stood Kenny as handsome as ever with teddy bears, gifts and balloons for baby Lisa. "Come in," said Auddie.

"I didn't know exactly what she needed or her size so I bought everything in two different colors and two different sizes. Can I see her Auddie? I promise you we'll talk after, and I'll make sure everything is crystal clear for you tonight."

Opening the door to her room he stood there with tears in his eyes as he stared at the child who certainly resembled him. "Why she looks just like me Auddie."

"I know Kenny...I know," as she went into the living room and he began to follow and began to open up to her.

"I know you have questions, but all I can say is I'm so very sorry, but this was my Dad...it was all about him and his reputation," said Kenny.

"And what about my reputation?" Auddie yelled back. "Did you once think about me? Your baby? Granny and I have been ousted from the church; the very church we'd been a part of for years. You never called, not once to check on either one of us. I couldn't use my scholarship because I was pregnant. And you say it's because it's about your Dad and his reputation. Take some responsibility for this Kenny!"

But as she went on to say another word, Kenny grabbed her and kissed her in his arms and carried her to her room.

"This can't be happening again." This is the one place, and the one man she promised herself never again. "But tonight I'll be his because I know he cares about me and his child. At least I hope this was a step in the right direction, and promises can be broken at least for tonight."

33

# Chapter Six

Shopping for Baby Lisa's first Valentine's Day was the only thing on Auddie's mind as she reached the store she worked in. She picked up musical teddy bears, and a box of candy, and a beautiful card for a Grandmother whose love for her never ceased. Auddie knew her Grandmother loved her and Baby Lisa unconditionally, more and more each day. However, feeling a little nausea as she was that morning, she decided to pick up a home pregnancy test just to make sure and to ease her mind.

After taking the pregnancy test early the next morning, she decided to present Granny with her Valentine's gifts first, but the smell of bacon that is usually in the air wasn't. Granny must've overslept. So Auddie dragged herself down to the kitchen to at least start cooking; that's the least she could do...she thought.

Once the kitchen was beautifully decorated with balloons and gifts, Auddie then decided to prepare Granny's favorite breakfast which was beef sausages, grits, waffles and her eggs scrambled soft, just the way she liked them.

Going back up stairs to check on Baby Lisa, who was still fast asleep, Auddie then went into Granny's room, "Happy Valentine's Day Granny." As Auddie drew closer to her bed, she was faced with one more of life's setbacks, for Granny Williams was dead...apparently she had died in her sleep.

Whatsmore the pregnancy test that she took earlier that morning read, 'positive'.

No one could possibly understand the magnitude of Auddie's love for her grandmother; nor the depth of her grief. For she was more than her granny, she was her protector and her provider, who always had her back; and the love, no greater love could one young woman possibly have for another person than Auddie had for her grandmother. And Granny told her of her love all of her young life. Whatsmore, she showered her with love. But what stands out to Auddie more than anything, was that her precious grandmother showed her in so many ways, just how much she loved not only her, but Baby Lisa too.

"My Granny's dead. Who's going to love me now? She's gone right when I needed her the most," Auddie said over and over to herself.

Mrs. Hattie Williams' home going service at her church St. Luke's Missionary Baptist was full to capacity. Even some of the saints from Reverend Kendrick Nelson, Sr.'s church came to lend support, but not the Reverend Nelson, nor his son was in attendance. But, Mrs. Nelson was there, and again whispered to Auddie (who was clearly distraught over Granny) and said, "I love you Australia and I'll always be here for you and the baby," and then handed her a card with a very sizable check.

Seven months later on September 27th, Madeline Annette Williams entered the world at 7 lbs 14½ ounces at 2:47am. And once again the pressures of Auddie's past, her fear and all her tears became her fortress of comfort. She awakened to them every morning and they rocked her to sleep every night.

Kenny in the meantime became the Assistant Pastor alongside his father and reaching out to him became an impossible task as all lines of communications, even to the church, were now blocked or numbers were changed. Auddie now with two babies she found solace in anything that had the letters G-I-N on the bottle.

Auddie was denied the privilege of having her daughters' christening at the church that used to welcome her with open arms every Sunday. This caused her to drown even further in her pain of guilt with more and more gin. And yet those very same folks elevated Kenny, but denied her any further membership. Auddie upset as she poured herself another shot or glass of whatever gin she could afford thought, "Why am I looked down on like this? It took the both of us to make these babies." Auddie questioned herself over and over; then the tears of depression would flow.

But one day a change will come one day, Auddie would say to herself as a reminder of Grandma Williams' words to her. "A change will come and if not for me, I pray for my beautiful daughters. So Lord, hear my prayer, forgive me and let me one day see a change... a change one day Dear

Lord please hear my prayer," a weeping Auddie would cry out.

A few years later, while Auddie was playing detective she came across a number to Kenny's apartment off campus and called. The person answering the phone indicated that he was Kenny's roommate but that he wasn't there at the moment.

"Do you know when he'll be back?" the inquiring Auddie asked.

"Well, he's getting married today, so he won't be living here anymore. Who can I say is calling?" But Auddie just hung up and reached for her ole friend Seagrams, which had become her comfort and her only friend! And because of her excessive drinking, she lost Granny's home and needed to move to a less expensive apartment for her and the girls.

# *Chapter Seven*

Auddie's drinking became her only solace and because of it she moved several times. The girls now school age were the one and only thing that she actually cared about and made sure they came home to a fairly clean home. A home cooked meal and she sat with them ensuring the importance of a good education every night. But once she retired to her room her dinner was Seagrams Gin, and her midnight snack was Absolute. This was not only her meal, this was her routine every single night.

Her latest move was to the Martin Luther King Co-op Apartments. The girls were now in high school. Lisa was a sophomore and Matty, a freshman, at the Rosa Parks School of the Arts. They both were very interested in vocals and anything to do with singing was the only quest that they liked and signed up for while at this school.

And as God will always place angels in our pathway so was the case when they moved again and their neighbor was Jenail Hightower, an Early Childhood Director/ Teacher of a childcare center; a divorcee raising twin daughters, Asia and Africa; who in turn became Auddie's girls' best friends, as Jenail and Auddie would be.

Jenail took notice immediately how Auddie would change the topic of conversation if the words church or better yet discussing their babies' daddies. Auddie would think of something and leave as quickly if Jenail kept talking about either one.

One day while Lisa and Matty were visiting, Jenail who knew not to ever question the girls couldn't help but to ask. So while they were listening and dancing and of course even singing, Jenail approached the topic very gingerly. "Hi ladies," Jenail said opening the bedroom door of her daughters' room. "I brought you all some refreshments. But I must admit you girls sound really good. You're parents must have that talent too right?"

Lisa answering first, "Our mom sang in church, but we don't know our dad."

"Oh I'm sorry. He's missing out and your mom is lucky to have you two wonderful ladies."

"Thanks Mrs. Hightower," Matty responded.

"We're having the youth in our church hold the entire service on Sunday. Do you think you girls would like to come?"

"Sure," said Lisa.

"Good. What about your mom?"

"Ah...Mrs. Hightower, please don't mention church to her," said Matty.

"Why?" questioned Jenail.

"All we know is she gets upset and closes herself up in her room."

"Oh my!" was Jenail's answer. "It's more serious than I thought."

Jenail after all was a good soul. She was a helpful neighbor willing to assist anyone in need. What's more, she had a smile that could light up anyone's bad or questionable day. But more than that Jenail loved the Lord and she could pray and believe for a breakthrough for the most harden of hearts. She also was a faithful member of the Neighborhood Baptist Church where the Reverend Kendrick Nelson, Sr. and his son were the presiding ministers.

The girls, Lisa and Matty, did go to the church with Jenail and her daughters the following Sunday and in time joined the church and the youth choir just like their friends. But, although Auddie could never attend she loved knowing the girls were in church. And she could never expose her painful secret to them. So she once again went on a drinking binge all by herself at the very thought of them finding out.

## *Charter Eight*

Auddie really tried to keep herself to-gether and not be so depressed by enrolling into school, but upon hearing that Kenny was elevated to Pastor after his dad's heart attack, she often asked, "Why am I looked down on and he gets promoted over and over again? Didn't it take both of us to make these babies?" Auddie pressed herself with that question as she had done a thousand times; then the tears would flow because in her world no one seemed to understand and if they did, they had no answers.

"But, one day a change will come", Auddie would say to herself as a reminder of Grandma Williams' words to her yet again. "A change will come and if not by me, I pray by my beautiful daughters. So Lord, hear my prayer, forgive me and let me one day see a change...a change...Lord, a change."

Auddie was a B+ student at the Community College, but started failing, failing to the point of dropping out. Later, she tried her hand in a real estate course, and just as she was to receive her license, she heard yet again news of Kenny. This time the church was honoring him and his wife with a brand new Mercedes-Benz. Auddie never received her Real Estate license because she lost sight of what was important. She lost her sense of who she was and what she wanted. She had a task however to aid her Broker, in whose trust he placed in her, but following the news of Kenny and his wife, she forgot to place the bid for a certain listed property for her boss. Instead, Auddie sat in her car by the side of the road crying. She lost the bid and her job as well.

The congregation grew and the choir was stronger than ever. As all four girls became soloists for nearly every song that was sung during the Sunday services. People were coming out more; the spirit in their hearts could be heard in every note. Auddie, who may have wanted to go, and several times she even got dressed drove herself to the church but the painful memories of a conversation between the Rev Kendrick Sr. and her granny were right there. Before she knew it, she was driving back home. She was told not to ever come back there and those words could never be easily erased. They were like a knife piercing her heart.

Jenail often prayed for her friend. She prayed that Auddie would allow herself the time to love and to heal as her daughters loved her. Jenail was placed over the women's Wednesday night fellowship and decided to bring the Women's Fellowship to her home and invite Auddie over. Auddie loved these meetings and would be in attendance every Wednesday evening at 7pm sharp. She found out by attending that God never leaves us, but it's folks who have issues such as her fears that walk away from God. Whenever we learn to give our fears to Him, he will step in to rescue us.

One cold November Wednesday evening as Auddie was greeting the ladies at Jenail's home and taking their coats, the doorbell rang. Auddie opened the door, and there stood the Pastor Kendrick Nelson, Jr. and his wife, and for the first time in fifteen years their eyes locked. Auddie seeing them standing there hand in hand was all she needed to see. She quickly excused herself and made a bee-line to the back door. Only this time her one true friend ran after her.

"Okay, hold up lady, where do you think you are going?"

"What's going on?" the inquiring Jenail asked.

"I just have to go.  Is anything wrong with that?"

"I know you feel you have to leave, I'm asking you why?" catching up to her and holding onto Auddie with all her might. Looking at her friend eye to eye she said, "Auddie, I'm your friend and whatever you've been running from, whatever you've been holding onto, whatever it is that has you up one day and down the next; I'm asking you, no, I'm telling you, for the sake of your beautiful daughters and for your own sanity, girl let it go for once and for all!"

Auddie looked up at her friend with huge crocodile tears rolling down her cheeks. "Your Pastor Kendrick Nelson, Jr. is the father of BOTH my girls!!" Auddie shouted. "The Pastor of the very church I grew up in and sang in every choir, but once I became pregnant I was told not to come back to resign; resign from everything I ever held there.  He gets promoted, but I must resign. The same folks that exiled me, promoted him, over and over again!!"

Jenail, who now understood the reasons behind her friend's mood swings, had tears rolling down her cheeks. "Well as my bible tells me that promotion comes from God. You can no longer run nor hide. The ole gospel song says, Look to Jesus, for it is Jesus who will see you through. Now, take my hand. Let's go back inside. You're running away for the last time."

"Please Jenail, I will. I promise, but not today," pleaded Auddie.

"OK, but right here right and right now we will pray. Father, today I thank You for all You've done for me and my family, most of all I thank You for my friend and her daughters that she has raised totally by your grace. Today Father, I pray that You will give her the courage to stand...to stand for You if she can't see herself standing for anything else. I pray that You will fill her life with love for everyone who has ever hurt her, and to know You will be with her to heal the disappointments she's borne all of these years. For all have sent her away- Lord, today give her peace to know she still has a purpose to fulfill; that there still lies a winner within her. For in You there are only winners, if she dare believe. This is my prayer in Jesus' name, Amen."

With that they hugged, and Auddie went into the confines of her home and to her room, where she cried in her pillow. She cried again, but this time, shedding thankful tears for the healing and for providing hope through Jesus to fulfill the purpose of her life to come.

That was the day when Auddie began to change her life. She began going and later joined Thy Will Be Done Pentecostal Church, and found God was always near. Her prayer life had grown and she held prayer and

Bible meetings in her home and her girl-friend and mentor Jenail remained loyal to her friend and was glad within her soul that Auddie had broken through the cocoon she had been in for far too long and so were her daughters

Auddie had even been given the position of Secretary to the church and handled that job with precision, making sure the Bishop Lenox Matthews had his notes typed, programs for Sunday service prepared, and funds banked if the Deacons were not available and the Bishop knew if Auddie was in charge it would get done without a doubt. His dependability of her was as mutual as her admiration of this tall well built, well-dressed, single overseer as well.

# *Part II*
# *Song Birds*

# *Chapter One*

By now the four friends were all juniors and seniors in Rosa Parks School of the Arts, practicing after school every day, in preparation of the biggest talent show of the year. In fact, J. P. Morris, one of the most famous record producers was going to serve as a guest judge.

They knew what they were going to wear and what song they were going to do when Lisa had come and said, "Last night after I said my prayers, and finally fell asleep. I was awakened with this song and I wrote it and we need to practice it because I feel it will give us the points needed to win because it is an original song, but it's truly a gift from God."

Matty looked at her sister and shook her head and said, "Another song? What's it called?"

"If I Only Knew Then, What I Know Now," she answered as she began to sing.

All the girls nodded while listening to Lisa sing and they all agreed that it would be the only one they would sing.

As the day approached, the outfits were taken to the cleaners. Their champagne colored pant suits, and the leopard print heels would give those suits that extra kick. Matty, the funniest and most fashionable of all four girls, certainly had the right position in helping to select the clothes. Asia was the most opinionated of the group, but was the one who actually selected the shoes. Africa was indeed the most laid back and was always the neutralist of the group. But when it came to Lisa, she was certainly the most optimistic of the group. She was also the most prayerful, and always sought God in her trials and this was one of those times.

As the program opened and the girls were backstage, their mothers were putting the final touches on their hairstyles, before they left for the auditorium to their seats. The stage manager came to the girls and informed them that they never gave a name for their group, and because of that they could not go on next. The girls threw out names but the vote was never unanimous, but when the name "Voices for Christ" was shouted out by Lisa, it was an instant winner. Everyone loved it.

It was now their turn and they were the last act. They held hands and was led in prayer by Lisa and then found their place on stage. Once the curtain opened the girls looking absolutely amazing and the sound of their voices intermingling one with another, it was magic; the way they all came together with that song. When it was over the audience went wild.

At the judges table, J. P. Morris had his mind and vote set on the last group, and nothing else would change his mind. The rest of the judges had to agree they would be the winners.

As all the contestants stood onstage, the principal Mr. White, and J. P. Morris first thanked everyone who came out in support of the Arts at the school, and also for the hard work each contestant had endured in preparation of this the greatest show ever held there this far.   Mr. White then started describing the winning prizes for the dance troupes, their prize would be to perform with the world famous Alvin Ailey Dance Company; for the winning musician he or she would play with the New York symphony for one week and the winning singers would record with J. P. Morris' company.

The audience went wild at the hearing of all the prizes.  The winning names were called, "James Turner, for his artistic dance. Susan Brown, for her drum set solo and for the singing segment..." J. P. Morris then said, "Voices for Christ."

Everyone was on their feet, screaming and shouting, "Go Voices!"

The "Voices for Christ" just stood, eyes closed and holding hands. J. P. Morris placed a card in each girl's hand which included a date and time and in his own hand the words "Don't be late!"

The girl's hugged and cried on stage while their mothers did the very same in the audience.

"Ladies, after all that singing I'm ready for Ms. Williams' good ole fried chicken...You?" Asia asked walking toward their parents.

"Of course, count me in," the girls responded.

## Chapter Two

As the girl's prepared for their meeting with J. P. Morris, he was already meeting with his team. They already had a plan and he sat at the head of his conference table with Big Mike his right hand and partner, Sasha the Secretary of this enterprise and the Reverend Kendrick Nelson, Jr. his silent partner. They sat listening as J. P. spoke of recording no more than two gospel tracks on their CD and from that point on it was going to go into a cross-over into R&B.

"But..." Sasha called out. "They're a gospel group. How are you going to get them to do that?"

J. P. looking over at her with his custom made Brooks Brothers' suit, Louie Vuitton shades and a Cuban cigar, peeled his glasses down to look at Sasha. "That's a question you will need to find the answer to.

In fact it's the leader of this pack that needs to be convinced. Bring in the hand, the fingers will follow! That's always been my motto. Now get moving, all of you. Put a plan together, they're due here at 3 pm, and for the sake of your jobs it better be a plan they'll go for."

The four girls were driven to their appointment by Jenail, and Auddie was there as well. Asia wasn't the only one somewhat disappointed at the fact that the moms wanted to come in as well, and she expressed her feelings. "Mom listen, we're just going in to hear what he has to say."

Jenail responded, "You're teenagers without agents or lawyers, so remember, not to sign anything until you discuss things over with us, do you hear me?"

"Yes mom, I hear you," said Asia.

"Promise me young lady," Jenail said looking over at her daughter.

Asia answered turning to look out of the window, "I promise, I promise."

"No…We Promise," as they all broke out into a hearty laughter.

As each girl stepped into the building they walked over to the reception desk where a young woman sporting a huge Afro and pretty green eyes and the most velveteen coco complexion, asked, "May I help you?"

Asia being the designated spokesperson said, "Yes, we're here to see Mr. J. P. Morris."

"Oh yes, he's expecting you, follow me. By the way, I'm Sasha, as she started to rise from her seat.

Lisa calls out, "Excuse me Sasha, where's your ladies room?"

"Oh, right over there, the third door to your left. Call me when you're all finished and I'll announce you before going to his office," Sasha said sitting back in her chair.

"Certainly," Lisa started walking in the direction of the bathroom. As all four girls followed her into the ladies room, they all just held hands as Lisa led them in prayer.

"Father, we thank you this day for all you've done for us thus far. We ask for favor today to keep doing what we do best...being Voices for Christ. Amen"

Walking out they called to Sasha, "We're ready now."

Sasha pushed the button in the elevator to the 19th floor, as soft symphonic music softly played in the background. They walked down a huge marble hallway upon reaching the 19th floor until they reached the end to the most tremendous cherry colored oak doors. Sasha pressed numbers on the keyboard, and then pushed the door after hearing the sound of the click. To their left stood a statue of J. P. Morris and to their right a brass door plaque with the name J. P. Morris, President of Morris and Morris Recording Company.

As the girls stood eyes glued to the plaque, Sasha's voice could be heard..."J. P., the Voices for Christ are here."

J. P.'s booming voice reached their ears, "Great! Send them right in."

Each girl stepped in wearing jeans, a black boyfriend jacket and touting their own favorite colored blouses; Lisa in lime and corresponding strappy heels; Matty in fuchsia and fuchsia heels; Asia in red and red heels and Africa in orange and orange heels. Big Mike and J. P. stood pointing to empty chairs and asked the girls to sit anywhere.

"Sasha, bring our guests some refreshments, Pepsi, Sprite, Grape or Orange?"

As the girls proceeded to give Sasha their choice J. P. started the meeting.

J. P. turned his attention to the quartet. "Well let's get the introductions out of the way."

"I'm Lisa."

"I'm Matty"

"I'm Asia"

"I'm Africa"

J. P. smiled with his approval. "Well, OK now, we've got the representation from the 'Motherland'."

Everyone broke out into a hearty laugh.

J. P. turned and introduced his partner and secretary, "This is my partner Big Mike, and Sasha. And I am the President, J. P. Morris, live and in Technicolor.

"Ladies you blew me away with your voices at the event last week. How long have you been singing together?"

"We're neighbors and we go to the same High School…"

"I see…neighbors, friendship and classmates that make beautiful music together. Well, we here at Morris and Morris Recording are always looking for new talent constantly and we think that your talent if changed a bit can reach many, many youth."

"Mr. Morris, our focus first of all is to sing to the glory of God and second to go to college. This 'change a bit' consists of what exactly? Singing secular music? We're strictly a gospel grounded group reaching souls for the Lord…and Only Him." Lisa stressed trying to project a confident and mature impression.

"Now let me tell you what's on my mind. This company, its rights and everything belong to me. I've been holding this place together for 15 years. We're always looking for up and coming artists. Since you won the singing segment last month, we would love to sign you on. We will give each of you $2,000.00 up front and cut you a track. Since you're teenagers and under-age, we'll provide you with an agent, and a lawyer and both will talk to your parents. We'll have you reaching souls with your music just like Mary, Mary."

Lisa feeling uncomfortable interrupts, "Excuse me Mr. Morris. We've been singing gospel since we were in grammar school, and we never were in it for the money."

Matty mumbles, "Speak for yourself."

J. P. winked at Big Mike...they just found their weakest link.

# Chapter Three

Three weeks later, sweet talking Mike went to the Rosa Parks High School pretending to be the uncle of Matty and Lisa. He said he needed to see Matty because he was locked out and needed the key to get in. The secretary asked him for identification and photocopied it; then called for Matty.

"What are you doing here?" Matty asked recognizing Big Mike by his size and his beautiful hazel brown eyes.

"Baby girl, I think you're the prettiest girl in the group. We protect our ladies," Mike stated quietly as they walked through the halls.

"We're not a part of your company yet," Matty reminded.

"I'm liking what I see and just wanted you to know I'm looking after you...if that is that okay with you?" he asked stopping and giving her his best stare.

"Yes, it's fine but why are you here?" Matty asked curiously.

"Just keep this between me and you. Is that okay?" Mike asked gently placing his huge hand on her shoulder.

"What about my sister? I tell her everything," Matty asked.

"Everything? You're kidding" he said.

"Everything," Matty repeated. "She's my everything."

"Now I am," Big Mike said as he picked up her hand, and kissed it and walked away. "See you at rehearsal." he called."

As the days turned into weeks and weeks became months, the courtship continued between Matty and Big Mike. Every other day she received flowers, night club tickets and theater show tickets. He knew he was stretching it a bit, but there was something so deep within her that it had him keep coming back to her school for more. And she would be more than willing to leave class altogether just to be with him.

Instead of making rehearsals, she was with Big Mike. And Big Mike had not been told to stop by Morris, so he was going to go as far as he could tonight. Why, Big Mike would go as far as it takes to help win her over to R&B music. Upon his date with Matty in which he spoke to her about the money and the glitz in one of Morris's limos and telling her all of this could be hers, if she would convince her sister; who basically runs the group to just do one track singing R&B music.

"Well," answered Matty. "I can only try."

"Well how's a full makeover and $7,000.00 credit card, to start with today?"

"Well," shouted Matty. "Say no more. I'm in! So let's go shopping!"

Taking the attendance sheets to the office for her English Literature class, the secretary known to all as Miss Carol approached Lisa while she was coming out of the Principals office.

She called out to Lisa, "by the way Lisa, please tell your parents if they want your uncle to pick up Matty, I will need a note from them."

"What uncle?" Lisa responded.

"Why your Uncle Michael...Such a looker that one. If I were about fifteen years younger I'd give him a second look myself," Lisa was still stuck on stupid at the phrases "Uncle Michael" and "picking up Matty."

Repeating what she just heard over in her head, "By the way Lisa, please tell your parents if they want your uncle to pick up Matty, I will need a note from them."

"How long ago did they leave?" Lisa finally asked.

"Oh, its about the same time every Monday and Friday and an occasional Wednesday."

"Did they happen to mention exactly where they were going?"

"Oh yes, her doctor's appointment," Miss Carol said.

"Oh yes, her doctor's appointment, I'll remind my folks tonight Miss Carol thanks. By the way do you remember when he first started picking her up?" Lisa asked.

"Oh sure honey, he's a looker; how can I forget it started about two months ago today"

Being very confused and border line angry, Lisa decided to call an emergency meeting with all the girls, so she started texting and hoped after she's done it that none of their teachers would confiscate their cells phones. But this was an emergency and Matty needed a reality check.

Matty was the first to text back as she replied "count me there." Asia and Africa texted back as well. Tonight was going to get pretty heated, but answers were needed and fast. At 6:00 pm all the girls were present, as Lisa lay on her face praying for God to give her the strength to say what needs to be said as well as the strength to hear what she knows may break up the group before they even got started. Lisa opened up her bedroom door and slowly walked down the long hallway of her home to the living room.

Asia started asking Matty, "Ok, what's up and where were you at 7th period?"

"Hi my ladies," Lisa said.

Matty sat legs cross and putting on lip gloss totally uninterested.

Lisa said, "Well, I called this meeting because I feel like we are not the group we all 'think' we are."

As the girls sat looking at each other, Matty said "Look, there are a million things I could be doing but I am here. They're here, say what's on your mind."

Lisa looked at Matty and said, "You Matty...You and your Uncle Michael. Why not tell all of us why Big Mike is picking you up during school hours? How could you put yourself and us, this group in jeopardy like that?"

"Look! I'm not doing a thing to you, and what I do with Big Mike let's say he counts for my million and one things to do."

"Matty, don't you know that it's a set up?" Lisa questioned

Africa finally said, "Wait. Take it back a moment. Is what you're saying is she's seeing Big Mike? Morris' Mike?"

"Don't you know Matty's been running around with her Uncle Mike who's been picking her up, taking her who knows where and doing...God only knows what and they have been at it for two months!" Lisa said to her friend.

Asia put her hands on her hip and gestured toward Matty. "Girl, listen to your sister, it's a set up, S-E-T-U-P!"

"What's more, what would Mama think? Are you so needy that you would ever think that he wants you for you? What's in it for us?" Lisa asked.

"No. What's in it for you?" Africa corrected.

Matty still fussing with lip gloss, calmly, almost like a whisper said, "He wants us to forget about singing Gospel and go into

R&B. Big Mike says every good singer has to do R&B first to get a following."

"To get a following!? Are you kidding me? This is a Gospel group Matty and that's that," Lisa reminded her.

"So now you're speaking for all of us?" Matty stood up and said.

"OK, it's fine with us," Africa and Asia announced.

"I'm speaking now, so listen up. This is the deal. He wants us to go R&B," Matty repeated. "And I want it too."

Lisa shook her head, not believing what she was hearing. "What is with her with all this, He wants…He wants us? He doesn't want just her. He wants you to turn on us. So we can do exactly what he wants. But what she forgot is whose life will we be a representative of if we do this? Who would you have to go against for what he wants?"

Lisa starts to sing "All To Thee My Precious Saviour I Surrender All". Matty storms out.

"But what if Morris does have our best interest?" asked Africa.

"Well here's my suggestion Africa, let's all meet here next week, same time and we'll take a vote. We'll vote on who's staying and who's leaving and that will be that. I'll tell Matty myself, and if you could do me one more favor, just one for next week."

"Sure. Ask," Africa shook her head.

"Of course, anything," Asia said.

"Promise me you will seek the face of God first before you come?" Lisa asked.

They all hugged and departed.

One week later Matty was the first to show up, and when the twins arrived they were surprised to know that Matty knew of an upcoming event in which they would be performing. So upon Lisa's arrival the twins approached her about a paid event that they knew nothing about.

Lisa took a seat and said, "Matty you have news about something?"

"Well, I overheard Mr. Morris on the phone and he was talking about us girl. Lighten up. It sounded real tight."

"Are you aware that we never signed a contract? Or even had another meeting with Mr. Morris?" Lisa asked.

"But we do," Matty replied.

"We do what?" Lisa asked not sure she understood Matty.

"We have a guaranteed meeting with a new recording deal to sign," Matty answered.

"What?" the twins said.

"Listen first things first. Are we all singing together or what?" Lisa asked.

Matty said with confidence, "Sure we are."

She reminisced about what Big Mike told her, "Just get them to sign and that's my ticket to your solo career."

"Hello babe can't talk long. I'm in the bathroom. I'm close. These girls are going to sign, baby," Matty assured him.

"Have they?" Mike asked. He knew until they do there was no guarantee things would go his way.

"Well no. Not yet. I did say I was close though."

"Close is not close enough. So step on it. My ass is on the line and that means yours too," he reminded her.

"OK I get it. Call you later, gotta go," Matty answered.

"Remember what we talked about Matty. All your dreams are about to come true," he reminded her.

"I got it babe," Matty said and hangs up.

"I hope you do...I really hope you do," Big Mike says as he hung up.

Matty walks back into the room.

"OK ladies, let's first think of our possibilities that's going to come out of all of this for us," Matty said as she sat down.

"Name some of them Matty, because I really have some doubts," Lisa said.

"But we don't," Africa countered.

"Oh, so I'm the hold up this time," Lisa said looking from Africa to Asia.

"I guess you are," Asia said sitting closer to her sister.

"OK I'm in, but I'm really having doubts," Lisa said finally.

"Great! I'll call Mr. Morris and set it up...See ya later," Matty gave Lisa a big hug and a thumbs up to Africa and Asia. They were on their way...but were they?

# Chapter Four

The contracts were signed the next day, and Mr. Morris started the girls in his studio making demos. The girls continued singing gospels.

Ladies do you think you can sing that song with a little bit more soul? Up the tempo or something…it's just not sounding right from here…right boys?

The soundman said, "Needs something boss, you're right."

"Listen, if we sing it with a beat, it's going to be just another R&B song," Lisa said beginning to feel a bit uneasy.

"Well Lisa, maybe that's what we need for you gals to be just a bit more soulful. You can always sing gospel down the line…but let's change this…"

"Tune?" Lisa asked.

"Tune, tempo. Why the song is all wrong for you anyway. Take these sheets, practice and come in on Friday and be ready to make this happen. For your folks, for you and huh...for me," Mr. Morris said with a smirk looking at the sound engineer.

Friday the girls were not ready and asked for a few more days. The day finally arrived and all the girls were there except Matty...two hours later she arrived.

"Where have you been?" Lisa asked walking her into the next available empty office.

"Lisa, we're not ready. I'm not ready and you know it," Matty expressed leaning against some cabinet.

"Would one of you like to find your friends and remind them that time is money," Mr. Morris said looking at his watch.

The twins went in search of Matty and Lisa.

"Here Mike," Mr. Morris said, "give this to Matty and calm her down right now." He withdrew a small white packet from his pocket and handed it to Big Mike.

"Hey are you sure boss? What about Lisa? She watches over them like a hawk."

"Let me handle Lisa. These girls are our next big success and we...no I won't let anyone or anything mess that up. One snort and my little songbird will sing all night long."

Big Mike knocks on the door, where the girls now have gone, and tells them Mr. Morris wants to see them. One by one they exit—but when Matty exits, Big Mike makes his move. "Matty let me holler at you one moment."

"Yeah what?" Matty asks.

"You some kind of nervous girly."

Matty crossed her arms, "You tellin' me. This is all happening so fast. I guess I just got overwhelmed. I don't know all the words or anything."

"How come? What could have been so important?" Mike asked.

"US History test…duh!!" Matty showing Mike that in spite of their relationship, she was still a kid.

"Okay cool. Look here Matty you need something to calm you right down," Mike said as he pulled out the little wide packet.

"I think you're right. What you got a beer?" Matty asked.

Mike laughed and said, "No, no beer, but how about a sweet high." He unfolds the paper and snorts first then hands it to

Matty. Without hesitation, because it's Big Mike, she does the same.

"Oh," she says and puts her hand on her nose.

"You okay babe?" Mike asks looking into her face.

"Yeah, I guess." Matty answers.

Big Mike begins to kiss her passionately and says, "And there's more of that just for you babe. Now you feeling me?"

"I'm feeling something, but what I can't explain," Matty says with a slight giggle.

Mike and Matty walk into the room where the others await. Big Mike and Mr. Morris touch knuckles and wink.

"You okay girl?" Lisa asks.

"Now? Sure!" Matty smiles.

"Let's take a minute to pray and then go over the words and our parts." The girls pray, while Matty laughs. They nail the song on the first take.

# *Chapter Five*

Meantime Auddie excited for her daughters, their recording contract and how things were working out for them, decided it's time for her to stop the blame game and join life. Truly her daughters shouldn't be her role models, she should be theirs. She was ready to make a change.

One day while at the church, Auddie received a call from Beth Israel Hospital. A private nurse for the Reverend Kendrick Nelson, Jr.'s mother in ICU was calling for her to come. The message to wait too long will be too late. Auddie, who owes Mrs. Nelson for all she's ever done for her and her girls down through the years, now was being called to come to her bedside. With the Reverend Nelson, Sr. already passed, all she had was her son and his family, but she loved Auddie and her girls as well. Upon reaching the ICU area Auddie prayed for God to go with her and before her to make a way of healing if it be His will.

Auddie kissed Ms. Ethel's forehead and asked, "Why didn't you call before now?"

Ms. Ethel smiled and said, "I called for you now because I didn't want you to talk me out of doing what I've done for you and your daughters and my granddaughters. I've done a lot in my lifetime and should God call me home, I'm leaving a third of my stocks to you and your girls."

"Oh no Ms. Ethel, you can't!" Auddie said.

"That's right Mom, what's wrong with you? Mom you should be ashamed of yourself," Reverend Kendrick Nelson, Jr. said walking in the room, looking at his mother in shock.

"No son, this woman raised your girls," his mother started getting excited and began coughing. "They're teenagers now and I've helped them every month of their young life. If anything you should be ashamed of yourself."

Rev. Kendrick took his mother's hand in his, "Mom, you're sick stop all this foolishness."

"You've been the fool son. You've fooled Auddie, her girls, the congregation but you can't fool me," Ms. Ethel said in as strong a voice as she could muster.

"Mom, what about me? What about my family?" He asked.

Coughing Ms. Ethel said, "You...Your family? They know me. I spent time with them, why, I lived with you all for years. But every month that those girls of Auddie's were born, I've visited with her every month just to be around my granddaughters...your daughters Junior, by pretending to be the Avon Lady just to see them. You and your Dad denied them, but God didn't and neither did I. Why, I've been more of a man to your children than you've been. So don't question my motives, son question yours."

During the next two weeks Auddie remained vigilant to the woman; who remained vigilant to her and her girls. She remembered the time rent was due and Ms. Ethel came by. When the electric was on borrowed time and time had run out, it was Ms. Ethel's perfect timing that stopped the deadline. Groceries needed…Ms. Ethel was there. She was always there.

And now Auddie has this time to finally do something for her. Brush her long beautiful white hair, lotion her legs or just to sit with her. Auddie never left her side but on March 28th at 8:40 am, Ms. Ethel looked at Auddie and she whispered something. Auddie placed her ear closer and heard her whispery voice say…"Love to all…Love to all."

And then she was gone. She sat with her while tears rolled down her face as she remembered a woman who would not allow herself to harden her heart. Finally, she pressed the button for the nurse. Auddie sat quietly as they unhooked the I.V., removed the pillow from under her head and covered her with a white sheet before rolling her to the morgue. As the nurse looked back at Auddie, she said, "I'm sorry for your loss." And Auddie just watched as the nurse along with Ms. Ethel disappeared behind the elevator doors.

Auddie got into her 2006 Altima, a gift to herself after she started back to work. Now she faced a whole new set of problems. How will she explain to her daughters that their grandmother died, when they never knew her?

Upon arriving home heart heavy, but so very grateful that Ms. Ethel was a woman of virtue. A true angel who truly loved her and her daughters and she had no reason to ever doubt it. Ms. Ethel was a true woman of God. She picked up the phone and first called the Bishop to help her with the how to go about talking to the girls. At 6:00 pm, Auddie and both daughters walked through the office of the Bishop Lenox Matthews, as they positioned themselves around his desk, the Bishop started a prayer.

"Father, today we look to you for guidance. We look to you because we know you know our hearts, our minds, our ability to know you are truth. As we approach this Pandora's Box, give us the heart to help them pass this hurt and as a family begins to heal. Thank you Father. In Jesus' name. Amen."

Matty looked at Lisa and said, "This looks serious, what's wrong? Better yet, who died?"

The Bishop looked at the girls and answered without hesitation, "Your grandmother."

Lisa looked at Matty and said, "We don't have one."

"OK listen girls. There was a time in my young life when Neighborhood Baptist was my life and then I became pregnant. I later became pregnant again from the same person, and he dropped me like a hot potato and his father told me in so many words I'll never be welcomed into that family and I'll never sing or be a part of that church, furthermore, I was not able to go back there again." Auddie rushed through her explanation and took a breath.

"What? Sounds like he's living so high and mighty, both him and his dad, that's all I have to say," Lisa was the first to speak.

Matty added, 'Sounds like they're both a..."

"Matty, watch yourself. So why are we all here?" asked Lisa.

"Because out of all of this, the one person who helped me financially and spiritually was his mother; she was your grandmother, and she passed today.

"But mom, I believe she meant a lot to you, but that means she was our dad's mom, so who was she?" Lisa asked.

Matty stopped her and interjected, "No! Who is he?"

Auddie looked from one to the other and said, "Your grandmother was my Avon lady, Ms. Ethel!!!"

Both girls yelled, "WHAT?"

"And her son is the Reverend Kendrick Nelson, Jr.," Auddie continued. "and he's your father.

"Girls, I just needed my Pastor here today for support. Because I was denied by him and his father, but Ms. Ethel never denied us, and she never missed a month coming by seeing you even if they told her not to. I'm not saying you have to like how they treated us, but she was different. She loved different, even if she had to pretend to be someone that she wasn't. So put your anger or whatever you may be feeling in check and come with me to her funeral."

The girls got up, hugged their mom and said, "Don't cry mom please. We get it. She loved us and showed you love. We'll be there," answered Lisa.

As the Bishop rose from his desk and held her as the girls hugged her, and said, "I'll be there for you too."

As the multitudes gathered at Neighborhood Baptist Church to get their last memory of Ms. Ethel, Auddie and Lisa sat in their living room patiently waiting for Matty. Auddie in a navy blue suit and an ivory colored blouse, and Lisa dressed in an ivory and black dress suit sat holding on to her mom's hand with all her might. The phone rang and the Bishop announced that he was outside.

Auddie grabbing her purse looked at Lisa and said, "Go tell your sister the Bishop is here OK? I'll meet you outside."

"OK," answered Lisa. Walking to Matty's room she yelled "Matty are you almost ready?"

"Sure am," answered Matty.

"OK, let's go then the Bishop is here."

"OK girl, go on I'll be right there I promise," Matty called out. Lisa leaves and as she opens the door of the Bishop's

Escalade, she turns quickly at the closing of the house door only to see Matty in a fire red pant suit.

"Oh my precious Lord," Auddie softly said.

"Sister Auddie, she's here. She's going and she's making a statement to the family who dismissed you and your daughters. Don't say anything to her, you too Lisa."

"But Bishop, she's going to embarrass us," Lisa said.

"Little Sis, don't you get it? No one will ever embarrass any of you again, and she's making mighty sure they don't forget any of you again."

When they finally arrived at the church the Bishop was ushered to the pulpit. Lisa went upstairs to the balcony. Auddie took a seat in the back, but Matty she walked right up front and found herself a seat among the rest of Ms. Ethel's family.

The home going service for Mrs. Ethel Nelson, widow of the Rev. Kendrick Nelson, Sr. and the mother of renowned minister, author, radio and television evangelist, the Rev. Kendrick Nelson, Jr. was memorable. Dignitaries from near and far came to this service and there were as many folks outside as there were inside. But it wasn't until the procession to view her for the last time that the girls sitting in two different areas started looking for their mother. This they both knew would not be easy for her. When they spotted her, both girls arose from their chairs and got to their mom's side. She must not go up there by herself.

As the line moved Matty held onto her mom's right hand and Lisa held on to her left. As the procession grew closer to the casket the girls could feel their mom's steps slowing down (almost faint like) her lips began to quiver until they found themselves looking into the face their mom's mentor, friend and life coach and their grandmother.

Kendrick stood hugging and shaking hands of the many mourners who came out to remember this woman who was celebrated in a way only the Neighborhood Baptist knew, songs of praise, shouting and praising the Lord, and in her favorite seating area a black and purple wrap laid a true testament of her life. As Auddie and the girls grew closer, eyes meeting for the first time since the hospital, he said "Thank you for coming."

Matty interrupted and spoke loud enough for all to hear, "Sorry for your loss, but we just found out the Avon lady was our grandmother, Dad. So for mistreating our mom, you can forget about any more recording deals with you and your team!"

"Stop it Matty!!" said Lisa. "This is not the time or place."

"Honey there could be no better place," Matty said. "Now let's get Momma outta here!!" Through conversations with Big Mike, Matty had found out that Rev. Kendrick was the silent partner of J. P. Morris.

And now with that, the girls still holding Auddie, walked out the church with the Bishop Lenox Matthews right behind them.

But when J. P. Morris came around to give his condolences he pulled Kendrick close so no one else could hear. "You better fix this and fast my man, and I mean fast," and he walked out as well.

As the many mourners walked around, Kendrick was standing in pure shock. The girls he voted for at a school talent show. The girls who were signed to J. P.'s company are his daughters. Now

J. P.'s giving him an ultimatum, but how can I fix this?

Kendrick's mind was racing for answers. "After all these years what is it that I can do now to do to fix this? After all J. P. is not the man anyone wants to cross."

As the days and weeks that followed Kendrick found himself alone, since his wife needed time to re-think who it was she actually married. And because of the scandal, the church had asked for his resignation, and then it was J. P. who he still could not, and whose threats were growing worse at each passing day.

"How can I make this right? I'm losing everything that ever mattered to me." Kenny would find himself saying.

# Chapter Six

Lisa hurt and bewildered went on to college and joined the college choir. Here she began traveling the world and was even lead singer on several of the songs. Lisa grew spiritually as she progressed in her new environment and continued to sing to His glory. Every weekend she spoke to Auddie and continued to hear how Matty had come to the house with her eyes blackened, or high on drugs given to her by Mike, who she now lived with.

The group Matty sang with only made two releases and neither one reached the charts or radio. They made a few highlighting debuts but nothing that made headline news anywhere.

The last conversation they had was at a friend's repass and Asia shared, "If only I knew then what I know now, I wouldn't have allowed myself to throw our friendship away for a few dollars."

Lisa embraced her and said, "Anytime anything seems too good to be true it usually is."

Asia with tears in her eyes asked, "Tell me Lisa, what kept you so very grounded through this all? Why didn't you take the plunge with us?"

"I did, but not for worldly goods that glitter and certainly that do not shine. I took a plunge for Christ and I refused to go back because He's proven over and over and over to be just faithful. Because of my faith in Him my friends and even my only sister turned away from me. I guess it's like the Bishop said, "Favor ain't fair." Lisa answered "By the way where's Africa?"

Asia shook her head and said, "Don't know. I haven't heard from her in weeks. I know I heard she's walking the beat for her new beau Danny."

"What!!? Where!!?" Lisa asked trying to wrap her mind around this new information.

"Down on Straight Street somewhere and although I heard about it, I have never seen her; not once. I've travelled early mornings and late night and still I never see her," Asia answered.

"Have you ever asked anyone down there?" Lisa asked, her heart aching for Asia and Africa.

"Once, and he stole my purse, so I just drive around looking; I don't get out of my car anymore," Asia said despondently.

Lisa and Asia set a day and time to ride around to find Africa. On that day, they drove for hours when suddenly they spotted her on the arm of a tall man heading for the Night Spot. When they walked in they immediately walked over to her as she sat on the lap of one guy while drinking out of the glass of another. As they got close their approach was interrupted by a well-dressed woman arguing with one of the men.

The woman said, "So here you are."

The guy whose lap Africa was sitting on said, "Hey babe, this ain't even what you're thinking."

"No huh? Well what the hell is your tongue doing inside her mouth? Was it looking for a vowel?" she asked.

"No hon, you see…" Africa started.

"You just shut the hell up…" she said now looking at the guy. "So this is what keeps you from your home, your family and our bed?"

"Babe, look…listen," he sputtered.

106

The lady pulls a gun from her pocketbook and takes aim, "I'm tired of your bitches coming before me."

Africa gets up from his lap and says, "Lady, listen."

"Didn't I tell you to shut the hell up? Don't say one more word. I see you all made up like Halloween itself. So this is what you like now," she said pointing the gun at Africa. "Halloween bitches. You've had, let's see, teeny boppers, pre-med bitches, working class women, season class women...but Halloween? Truly you must be kidding."

He stood up, "Look, just let her go; it's me you're after right?"

"Yeah, it's him right?" Africa pleads.

The lady pulls the trigger and the gun fires. When all was said and done, Africa was bleeding on the floor of the dirty tavern.

"What did you do!!?" He grabbed the gun from her hand. "What did you do!!?"

She looked at her husband and said, "Why babe, I just got rid of Halloween, the least you can say is thank you," She then sat down and waited for the police to arrive

Lisa and Asia rushed to Africa's side. As she reached her sister's side and holds her hand, she hears, "I'm sorry." Africa dies before she could respond.

"No! No!" Asia cries.

Lisa comforts her friend and when it's all said and done, takes her home.

Feeling overly sad for her friends Asia and Africa, Lisa heads home. Her mother is in the living room. She walks over, sits down and puts her head in her mother's lap and begins to weep.

"Oh Mama, what's happening here? Why do I feel God has left us?" Lisa cries.

"My, my, listen to my child. Do you know why I supported you and Matty but couldn't go to the church? It's because when I would hear you sing...it reminded me of the life of singing I had, and how...Lord knows, how far I fell from grace. I supported you because I love both of you so much, but I fell so hard that I couldn't believe it. Then I was a mother and being your mother helped at times to heal my pains...but to answer your question, God never left us...but some-how we left Him."

Auddie stroked Lisa's back as she sang, "I Won't Complain."

"Lisa, remember when Asia told you, "If she only knew then what she knows now?" Auddie asked. "Well, that happens to be my story as well."

"Yours too?" Lisa asked.

"Mine too," Auddie answered.

## Chapter Seven

Lisa, home for the summer break, finds her mother in the kitchen fixing breakfast, "Mom, have you heard from Asia?"

"I wanted to wait until you got home, but Asia is in Passaic General," her mother answered. "I didn't want to worry you so I didn't tell you before."

After breakfast, Lisa went to the hospital to see her friend. "Asia, what happened? How did this happen?"

"Look, I couldn't tell you before," she started.

"Tell me what?" Lisa asked.

"I've got the virus," Asia answered.

"No!!!" Lisa exclaimed and began crying.

"Look, I need you to be strong. You've been the strongest out of the four of us, and I need you to be strong now," Asia said with tears streaming down her cheeks.

"Why couldn't you tell me?" Lisa asked.

"How does one start a conversation about oneself, and end that same conversation with the word 'A-I-D-S'? I was in total denial and it's the denial that's killing me. The fact is that I refused medical care, counseling assistance or anything that said AIDS. I put it off. I couldn't face anyone so, I just ignored it like it would just go away." Asia said interrupted by a series of coughs. "You're looking at someone who didn't think enough of herself to get help for herself."

"But how? Where?" Lisa was confused. No one she was close to ever contracted AIDS.

"It doesn't matter Lisa. Just know when my twin died, I died. So I needed to feel love. I needed someone to love me and I just kept testing the waters until I got more than I asked for."

Lisa crying softly said, "Oh Asia...I loved you...you're my best friend. Don't you know that?"

"I can't tell you how empty I felt without Africa. I was trying to fill a void I guess," Asia said coughing.

The nurse came into the room and said, "Visiting hours are over dear."

Lisa nodded, "Okay, I have to go Asia." Lisa hugged her and Asia continued to cough quietly.

As the days turned into months, Lisa and Asia were inseparable. Going to her doctor appointments, shopping, and movies; doing anything and everything they could together. As Asia grew weaker, Lisa grew

112

stronger in her faith. She prayed earnestly for her friend and mostly for Asia's mother who was now facing the fact that she was going to lose her last child. On one visit to Miss Jenail's, Jenail just hugged her. No words were spoken but Lisa knew she was grateful for her just being the best friend in the lives of both her daughters.

Packing up some things to take to the beach, Asia watched as Lisa carefully got everything for her friend. They talked about their long friendship, had hamburgers, French fries, even a cone and somehow as Lisa glanced at her friend; she almost looked more peaceful than she had ever been before. As the beachgoers began to leave, Lisa started rolling up towels and their lunch baskets.

"Stop, I want to stay until the sunset. I want to watch it today, Lisa for I may not have a chance like this again," Asia said.

"Are you in pain?" Lisa asked.

"No, but I've always wanted to see it, and girl, I can't be putting too many things off these days. You know? I know I'm running out of time, so be a friend and wrap up in my blanket and watch it with me," Asia said looking so weak and pale, but determined.

As the two sat sitting on the boardwalk watching the sunset, Lisa hugged her friend and she quietly sang, "How Great Is Our God". By the time they reached the city, Asia was shaking with fever. Lisa drove directly to the hospital where Asia lasted a little over a week before she expired.

# Chapter Eight

Lisa sat at the kitchen table with her mother, questioning how God has spared her life and allowed her to live as she asked.

"Why me, Mama?" She asked.

"He needs your testimony and praise. He only desires our praise," Auddie answered with wisdom.

"Mama, why couldn't Africa, Asia and even Matty just allow his praises to be enough?" She asked.

"He uses us all for different reasons. I can't answer for them child, I can only answer for myself," she answered.

The day of the funeral finally arrived. Friends and family near and far came to bid farewell to Asia. The church had standing room only. When the pastor finally stood and said, "Here lies one soul I groomed, but decided her way was best. Young people hear me, it's easy to get caught up with the world, but God only wants your praise. 'Choose ye this day whom ye shall serve.' I have been in constant communication with a sister here who has been called to the ministry. This was highly difficult for me to change the course of protocol in this church, but today I'm introducing to all of you for the first time ever; a woman who, in spite of her sister, and her best friends, continued to hold onto God's unchanging hand, Minister Lisa Williams.

In spite of the tears, the hurt and the pain of the day, the entire church stood and applauded her walk to the podium. Lisa spoke on the very words Asia gave to her months ago, "If I Only Knew Then, What I Know Now".

Auddie accompanied her dear friend Jenail home after the service. Jenail was so grateful to Bishop and Lisa for giving Asia such a beautiful home going celebration. They talked about the girls and examined the choices that the four had made.

Jenail had fallen victim to cancer. Auddie now would cook and clean Jenail's home and feed her every day. Yet every time she hugged her good bye, Jenail would say, bring me that fragrance you have on the next time you come. And everyday Auddie would say you can count on it.

Jenail had lost 2 daughters in a year's time and as Auddie sat with her friend, listening to her say how she wanted the fragrance Auddie was wearing; once again Auddie held her head and pointed towards her dresser. There stood over 70 bottles of Avon fragrances. Jenail could only say "you didn't forget." In three weeks Jenail had passed as well.

By the time of her home going service, the Bishop Lenox Matthews told Auddie her strength as a friend is what he needs in a wife, and asked her to marry him.  In all she had been through happiness finally was hers and she welcomed it.  And her life had meaning along with her prayer life and the love she found with her new husband.

# *Epilogue*

"Well that's it. That's our story. Remember it. It's my story, my life, my friends and the choices we all chose to walk. Tell it to your children," Octavia stands and gives Lisa a warm embrace. Her face is wet with tears of sorrow and joy.

The rest of Lisa's grandchildren come upstairs to see why it was taking them so long to bring the rest of the boxes down. They grabbed one or two boxes a piece and handed them off to the movers. Lisa put on her hat, shut off the light and closed the door. Reopening the door Lisa walks over to the chair, picks up the photo album and bible.

She hugs them to her chest and says, "Now, I'm ready."

# *About the Author*

Ms. Lois Dais-Kelley can easily be described as a woman of purpose. She is a worshipper, servant and intercessor who seeks the presence of god. She considers herself a woman who truly loves mentoring, ministry and motivational speaking.

Ms. Dais-Kelley has worked for the St. Joseph's Hospital of Paterson, New Jersey for over 20 years as a Senior Residential Staff which over see several group homes.

She is a powerful speaker and her topics range from the "Principal of Purpose" to "This is the Highway of Life But Where are You Going?" These are a must hear for every age.

Her degrees vary from Education, Public Speaking and African American Studies. She speaks often to schools, and churches and her motto: "Teach a child in the way that he should grow and when he grows it shall not depart from him."

Lois Dais-Kelley holds a doctorate in Theology.